2

# One Yak
# Called Jack

# for Pierre

ONE YAK CALLED JACK
A Jonathan Cape Book 0 224 04685 3

First published in Great Britain in 2005 by Jonathan Cape,
an imprint of Random House Children's Books

1 3 5 7 9 10 8 6 4 2

RANDOM HOUSE CHILDREN'S BOOKS
61–63 Uxbridge Road, London W5 5SA
A division of The Random House Group Ltd

RANDOM HOUSE AUSTRALIA (PTY) LTD
20 Alfred Street, Milsons Point, Sydney,
New South Wales 2061, Australia

RANDOM HOUSE NEW ZEALAND LTD
18 Poland Road, Glenfield, Auckland 10, New Zealand

RANDOM HOUSE (PTY) LTD
Endulini, 5A Jubilee Road, Parktown 2193, South Africa

THE RANDOM HOUSE GROUP Limited Reg. No. 954009
www.kidsatrandomhouse.co.uk

A CIP catalogue record for this book is available from the British Library.

Printed and bound in China

# Darcia LaBrosse

# One Yak Called Jack

JONATHAN CAPE
LONDON

'Hop on my back,'

said Jack.

'I'll take you to the fair

and back.'

'Ready, Ferrets?'

said Jack.

'Not yet!'
'After dinner, Jack.'

'Papa, Mama,
    Baby Crab!
On my back!'

'In a tad.'
'We're busy building, Jack.'

'Foxes, hop on!
To the fair and back,'
called Jack.

'Must run now.'
'But we'll be back.'

'Coming, Piggies?'

asked Jack.

'Not right away.'
'We're making hay.'

'Escargots!
Time to go!'

'Soon, Jack.'
'We're having a snack.'

'Monkeys, quick!'

cried Jack.

'In a tick.'
'We're scratching, Jack.'

'Seals!
Wake up!'

snapped Jack.

'After our nap.'
'We're snoozing, Jack.'

'Please,
Caterpillars,
ple-e-e-ase,

to the fair and back.'

'Hang on!'
'We're tied up, Jack.'

'Birdies, come on!

I'm leaving,' said Jack.

'Just a minute, just a sec.'
'Coming, coming, Jack!'

'Not fair!'
sighed Jack.

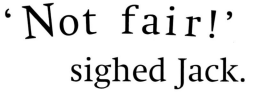

'Everybody's just too busy
to come with me.'

'But wait, Jack!'

'What?'

'We're ready *now*, old Yak!'

Hmmmm. Let's see . . .'

10 birds
9 caterpillars
8 seals
7 monkeys
6 snails
5 pigs
4 foxes
3 crabs
2 ferrets
2

and . . .

# 1
# Yak called Jack!

'But can **everyone** fit on my back?'